LOBSTAH GAHDEN

Speak out against pollution with a wicked awesome Boston accent!

WORDS BY
ALLI BRYDON & EG KELLER

PICTURES BY
EG KELLER

sourcebooks
eXplore

Walter was a proud lobstah.

His home: spotless.

His style: straight out of *Crustacean's Illustrated*.

His gahden: a blooming paradise!

Yes, Walter had quite the blue thumb.
He was hip to the latest underwater gahdening trends.

Native kelps!

Ornamental grasses!

Rainbow algae!

This careful crustacean was meticulous
in his maintenance.

Walter had one big dream:
to win the annual SWELL GAHDENS contest.

He worked hard all year long to keep a most
perfect lobstah's gahden.

Milton was loud.

He was chaotic.

And his gahden just flowed with the tides.

The judges ate it up!

This year, Walter would be #1!

But just as he was leveling his hedges...

He knew exactly who was responsible.

Of course, they worked it out like adults.

But it didn't stop.
Walter woke every morning to
another disgusting thing dropped in
his once-flawless gahden.

So did Milton.

Walter's sea grapes burst.
Milton's phytoplankton flipped.
And not in the good way.

Each blamed the other.
All the while, both gahdens
filled with garbage.

Then, one particularly
trashy afternoon...

The gahbage mountain tumbled down.

Clearly things had gotten out of claw.

"Milt, I think we found the culprit," said Walter.

"How's about we get a look topside?" said Walter.

"I was gonna suggest tha same thing," said Milton.

Milton and Walter hightailed it to the surface to take a look around.

"Milt, I gotta idea how ta solve what appeahs ta be a mutual problem," said Walter.

"I'm all antennae, Walt..."

It was the first time they
agreed on anything.

Walter and Milton eventually went back
to doing what they did best.

"That's some prizewinnin' sea cabbage."

"Wicked excellent eelgrass!"

Not everything changed.

But one thing
certainly did.

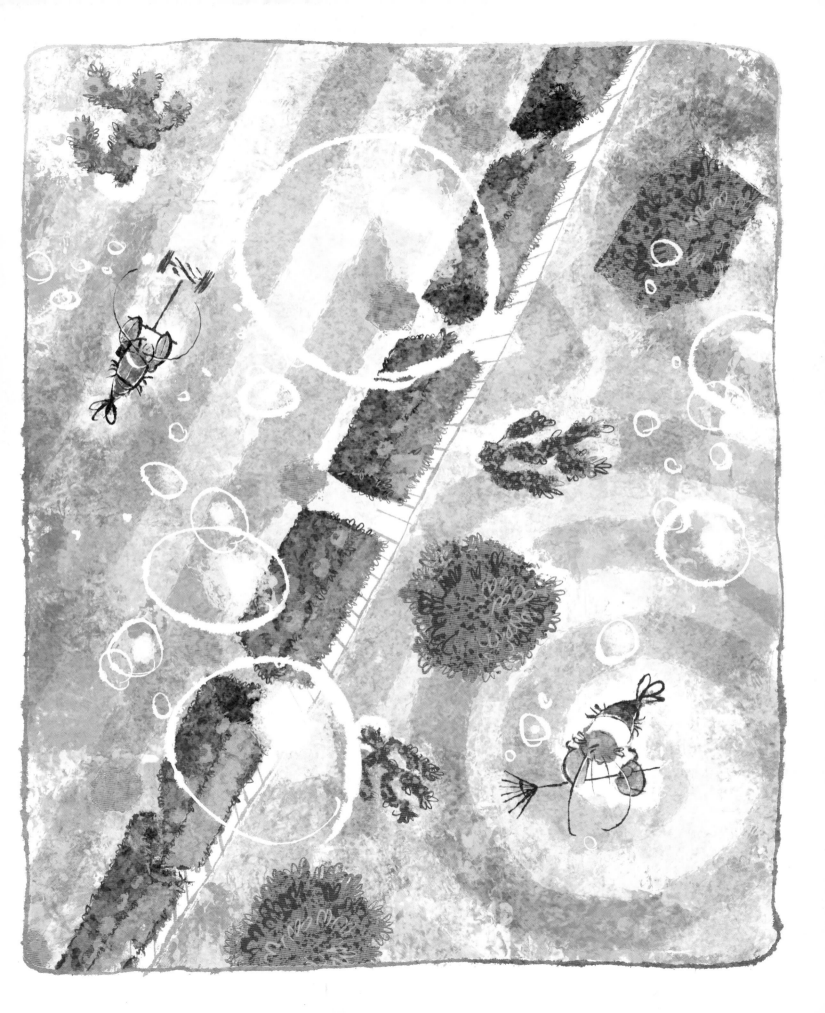

LOBSTAH KNOWLEDGE

World Wide Watah

Oceans cover more than 70% of our planet—that's a lotta watah! Scientists estimate that about one million species of underwater creatures live in our oceans, from the smallest plankton to the largest blue whale. Most of Earth's living beings actually live underwater, rather than on land. And more unique sea animals are discovered all the time, such as the rare blue lobster...like Walter!

Have you ever seen a clawed lobster, like our friends Walt and Milt, before? Lobsters are crustaceans, meaning they have a hard, outer shell called an exoskeleton. They also have ten legs that are jointed, or bendy at a point in the middle. Two of those legs have large, super-strong claws which lobsters use to crush and tear apart fish to eat. Their bodies are about 10–20 inches long, and end in a flat tail. The blue lobster, like Walter, is rare to find. Its blue color comes from a genetic mutation that makes them produce more of a certain protein.

Undah-watah Life

In this story, Walter and Milton live in the ocean and grow some pretty spectacular gardens there, filled with kelp, eelgrass, sea cabbage, and more. These plants are not only beautiful, but also helpful to those of us who live up on land. Did you know that sea plants make half of the oxygen that humans breathe?

The ocean is a wild and wonderful place, home to creatures you may already know—like lobsters, fish, whales, and sharks—and some that seem too strange to be true. For example, have you ever heard of a vampire squid, mantis shrimp, or mimic octopus? Go check them out—they're amazing!

Our oceans are colorful, vital, and diverse ecosystems, and we cannot live without them. But just like in Walter and Milton's fictional ocean home, humans pollute Earth's oceans daily. Billions of pounds of garbage and other pollutants go into the ocean *each year*. From single-use plastic, to leaking oil and detergents, to carbon emissions, and even noise pollution—humans are responsible for much of the oceans' decline. And our under-the-sea friends are at risk.

HOW CAN YOU HELP WALTER, MILTON, AND THEIR NEIGHBAHS?

- Reduce and/or recycle the plastic you use (like plastic straws, bags, toys, and bottles).
- Help clean up a coastline.
- Don't pour anything but water down the drain.
- Ask your parents to buy and cook fish that are sustainably sourced.
- Keep learning about the state of our oceans.
- And most importantly, talk about ocean care and conservation with your friends... and get them on board too!

These ah-ganizations are doing good things for Earth's oceans:

- **Ocean Conservancy**, oceanconservancy.org
- **Plastic Pollution Coalition**, plasticpollutioncoalition.org
- **Oceanic Preservation Society**, opsociety.org
- **Oceana**, oceana.org
- **Monterey Bay Aquarium Seafood Watch**, seafoodwatch.org

WICKED AH-SOME, KID!

You may have noticed that Walter and Milton talk a certain way. These lobsters hail from New England—off the coast of Boston, Massachusetts to be exact. So, they've picked up the famous Boston accent, which is a blend of accents from Britain (from English settlers in the 1600s) and Ireland (from Irish immigrants in the 1800s). The Boston accent and slang are particular to the city of Boston, but the rest of New England boasts variations on this accent.

If you want to speak like Walt and Milt, here are some tips: say the letter "r" like "ah" as in "watah" (water). You can also add an "r" to the end of certain words, like "dramar" (drama). When the sound "o" appears in the middle of a word, say it like "aw," as in "spawts" (sports).

Glawssary

Bawstin Hahbah (Boston Harbor): the body of watah where Milton and Walter live.

Barrel (garbage can): where yer supposed ta put yah gahbage (*instead of in the sea*)!

Bubblah (bubbler): what you might call a fish blowin' a lotta air. Just kidding! It's a water fountain.

Chowdah (chowder): a chunky soup filled with seafood. Make sure you order the one from up north: New England Clam Chowdah (white), *not* Manhattan Clam Chowder (red).

Fresh: what you want your fish to be. What you *don't* want your kiddos to be, i.e. "rude."

Idear (idea): the kind of genius plan that Walter & Milton dreamed up to solve their gahbage problem.

Lobstah pawt (lobster pot): a lobster trap.

Rawd (rod): what ya might fish with. Has a reel, line, and hook.

Smaht (smart): another way of saying "you gotta lotta brains in yer head, kid!"

Sub: not a submarine in the watah, but a wicked lahge sandwich.

Wicked: another way of saying "very," as in "wicked ah-some, kid."

References

BBC. "How Rare Are Bright Blue Lobsters?" Updated May 25, 2016. https://www.bbc.com/news/magazine-36369687.

BostInno. "Pahk the Cah in Hahvahd Yahd: Researchers Locate the Origins of the Boston Accent." Accessed August 7, 2020. https://www.americaninno.com/boston/pahk-the-cah-in-hahvahd-yahd-researchers-locate-the-origins-of-the-boston-accent/.

Hughes, Catherine D. National Geographic *Little Kids First Big Book of the Ocean*. Washington: National Geographic Society, 2013.

Ministry for the Environment. "What You Can Do to Protect Our Marine Environment." Accessed August 7, 2020. http://www.mfe.govt.nz/marine/marine-pages-kids/how-you-can-reduce-marine-pollution.

National Geographic Kids. "Ocean Habitat." Accessed August 7, 2020. https://kids.nationalgeographic.com/explore/nature/habitats/ocean.

National Oceanic and Atmospheric Administration. "Ocean Pollution." National Ocean Services website. Accessed August 7, 2020. http://www.noaa.gov/resource-collections/ocean-pollution.

National Oceanic and Atmospheric Administration. "How Many Species Live in the Ocean?" National Ocean Services website. Accessed August 7, 2020. https://oceanservice.noaa.gov/facts/ocean-species.html.

New England Historical Society. "How to Talk With a Boston Accent (Not For the Faint of Haht)." Accessed on August 7, 2020. https://www.newenglandhistoricalsociety.com/how-to-talk-with-a-boston-accent-not-for-the-faint-of-haht/.

Natural Resources Defense Council, Inc. "Ocean Pollution: The Dirty Facts." January 22, 2018. https://www.nrdc.org/stories/ocean-pollution-dirty-facts.

Oceanic Society. "7 Ways to Reduce Ocean Plastic Pollution Today." Updated July 28, 2020. https://www.oceanicsociety.org/blog/1720/7-ways-to-reduce-ocean-plastic-pollution-today.

The World. "Why is the Boston Accent So Wicked Hard?" March 6, 2016. https://www.pri.org/stories/2016-03-06/why-boston-accent-so-wicked-hard.

Time. "11 Lobster Facts That Will Leave You Shell Shocked." Updated July 8, 2015. https://time.com/3184569/11-lobster-facts-that-will-leave-you-shell-shocked/.

Universal HUB. "Pronunciation." Accessed on August 7, 2020. https://www.universalhub.com/glossary/pronunciation.html.

Universal HUB. Accessed on August 7, 2020. https://www.universalhub.com/glossary/a-b.

Wilsdon, Christina. *Ultimate Oceanpedia: The Most Complete Ocean Reference Ever*. Washington: National Geographic Society, 2016.

With special thanks to Maddie Frost and the Dowd Family,
Boston-area locals who consulted on the accent.

For Ed, who loves the sea as much as I do.

—AB

Text © 2021 by Alli Brydon and EG Keller

Illustrations © 2021 by EG Keller

Cover and internal design © 2021 by Sourcebooks

Sourcebooks and the colophon are registered trademarks of Sourcebooks.

The artist combined a variety of scanned paper and paint textures with Procreate on an iPad Pro to create the full color art.

Published by Sourcebooks eXplore, an imprint of Sourcebooks Kids

P.O. Box 4410, Naperville, Illinois 60567–4410

(630) 961-3900

sourcebookskids.com

Library of Congress Cataloging-in-Publication Data is on file with the publisher.

Source of Production: 1010 Printing Asia Limited, North Point, Hong Kong, China

Date of Production: December 2020

Run Number: 5020428

Printed and bound in China.

OGP 10 9 8 7 6 5 4 3 2 1